This **Aussie Kids** book belongs to

....

who lives in

....

For gorgeous Emma, Sienna and Stella. *B.M.*
For my wife May and kids, Caden and Summer. *D.H.*

PUFFIN BOOKS

UK | USA | Canada | Ireland | Australia
India | New Zealand | South Africa | China

Penguin
Random House
Australia

Penguin Random House Australia is part of the Penguin Random House group of
companies whose addresses can be found at global.penguinrandomhouse.com.

First published by Puffin Books, an imprint of
Penguin Random House Australia Pty Ltd, in 2020
Text copyright © Belinda Murrell 2020
Illustrations copyright © David Hardy 2020

Cover and internal illustrations by David Hardy
Design © Penguin Random House Australia Pty Ltd
Author photograph © Jen Bradley
Typeset in 18pt New Century Schoolbook by Midland Typesetters, Australia

Printed and bound in Australia by Griffin Press, part of Ovato

A catalogue record for this
book is available from the
National Library of Australia

NATIONAL
LIBRARY
OF AUSTRALIA

ISBN 978 1 76089 365 1

Penguin Random House Australia uses papers that are natural and
recyclable products, made from wood grown in sustainable forests. The logging
and manufacture processes are expected to conform to the environmental
regulations of the country of origin.

penguin.com.au

Aussie Kids

Meet Zoe and Zac at the Zoo

Belinda Murrell & David Hardy

PUFFIN BOOKS

Northern
Territory

Western
Australia

South
Australia

Australia
Queensland
New South Wales
ACT
Victoria
Tasmania
Come visit us in New South Wales
Hi! I'm Zoe
I'm Zac

POSTCARD

Hi,

We're Zoe and Zac and we're twins. Well, we're not really twins, but almost! We were born on the same day, in the same hospital in Dubbo. Our mums were in beds side by side. Now we live next door to each other, inside the zoo!

Zac and I are super lucky. There's always something exciting happening — especially today. We hope you can come and visit us. It will be the best adventure ever.

Zoe and Zac

FROM:

Zoe and Zac

Dubbo

New South Wales

Australia

Chapter 1

A Super-Special Saturday

Zoe was the luckiest girl in the world.

She lived at the zoo.

Her house was in a row of six cottages for zoo workers and their families.

It was hidden away behind
a belt of trees. Her best
friend Zac lived next door.

Wild animals, like
kangaroos, koalas and
emus visited their gardens
to feed.

From the kitchen window,
Zoe could spy giraffes and
zebras strolling across the
plain. She could even hear
the roar of lions and the
trumpeting of elephants.

Zoe loved her home.

'*Good* morning,' cried Zoe.

'Good morning, sweetie,' said Mum. She hugged Zoe. Her stepdad, James, was cooking.

'Yum,' said Zoe. 'That smells fantastic.'

'I thought you'd need a big breakfast today,' said James. He scooped a pile of scrambled eggs onto warm toast.

'Ready for a busy day?' asked Mum.

'Uh-huh,' said Zoe. 'I can't wait.'

Zoe was *super* excited about her seventh birthday treat. Today, Mum was taking her to help at the zoo.

Zoe was wearing her junior zookeeper's uniform. She had old brown shorts, a green shirt, Mum's old zookeeper cap and her sturdy boots.

Her backpack was filled with everything she might need for a day of zookeeping.

Best of all, Zoe's almost-twin Zac was coming. It was his birthday treat, too.

On Wednesday, Zoe and Zac had both turned seven. Mum said they were *finally* old enough to help her with the animals.

Zoe was ready to go!

She gulped her breakfast.

Just then Zac peered around the back door with his mum.

'Hi Zac,' cried Zoe. 'Hi Marlee. Come in.'

Toby the orphan wombat
woke up and butted the side
of his pen.

'Are you hungry, Toby?'
asked Zoe.

Toby grunted.

'Toby's *always* hungry,'
said Zac.

Zoe fetched a carrot. She
poked it through the bars.
The wombat crunched it up.
Chunks of carrot flew all
over the floor.

Zoe laughed.

'Let's go,' said Mum. 'We
have lots more hungry
animals to feed.'

Zoe and Zac jumped up.
What amazing animals
would they look after today?

Chapter 2

Amali

The sun shone out of a
clear sky. The warm breeze
smelled of gum trees and
dried grass. Mum drove the
jeep with the animal food
in the back. Lots of visitors
rode past on bicycles.

'I can't wait to feed the giraffes and cuddle the meerkats,' said Zoe.

'I can't wait to feed the elephants and cuddle the lions,' said Zac.

'We won't be cuddling any lions today,' said Mum. 'Or you might be their dinner!'

Zac gulped.

Zoe giggled.

Mum laughed.

First stop was the lions. They lived in a large enclosure like the African plains. Mum had an esky full of meat. The father lion roared. Zoe covered her ears.

'Coming, Zulu,' said Mum. 'Be patient.'

Six young lions charged for their breakfast. But the mother lioness turned away. She growled and stalked off towards the trees.

'Amali's not hungry,' said Zac.

'Lions are always hungry,' said Zoe.

'That's strange,' said Mum. 'Maybe she'll come soon.'

Mum fed the lions through a special chute in the safety fence. They growled and snarled.

'Can I give them some meat?' begged Zac. 'Please?'

Mum nodded with a smile. 'For a birthday treat. Come and stand right next to me.'

Zac put a chunk of meat in the chute and closed the hatch. The chunk plopped down on the other side.

Two young lions raced towards the fence. They grabbed the meat and pulled, like playing a game of tug of war.

Zulu roared again.

Zac could feel hot lion breath on his face.

'Amali still hasn't come,' said Zoe.

Mum looked around.

'Maybe she's scared of Zulu,' said Zac. 'He's *fierce*.'

'We'll come back later and check on her,' said Mum. 'We've lots to do.'

Chapter 3

Meerkat Mischief

The next stop was where the giraffes, eland and zebras roamed. Mum carried a bale of hay. Zac and Zoe carried another. They climbed up onto the viewing platform to feed the animals.

Nala, one of the giraffes, galloped over followed by her calf. Kanzi butted his mother with his head, then tripped over his own skinny legs.

'Kanzi's so clumsy,' said Zac, pretending to be a goofy baby giraffe.

Zoe giggled.

'He's just a baby,' she said. 'He'll soon be as fast as his mum.'

Zoe scooped up a crunchy carrot for Nala. The giraffe curled out her long, blue tongue and took the treat. Nala's knobbly tongue tickled Zoe's fingers.

'Now for the meerkats,'
said Mum. 'Stay close to me
while we go inside.'

'Can we really go in?'
asked Zoe.

She'd never been inside
with the meerkats before.

The meerkats lived in a
sandy enclosure.

One was standing on
a high rock watching for
danger. The meerkat's nose
twitched.

It hissed a warning. The
meerkats crowded around,
their noses twitching.

'Walk slowly and calmly,
and sit on the log,' said Mum.

Zoe and Zac walked
carefully inside.

As a zookeeper's daughter, Zoe knew how to behave around animals.

Zoe and Zac sat down.

Mum handed them each a bowl filled with wriggly grubs.

One meerkat climbed onto Zoe's lap. He gobbled a mouthful of grubs. Another climbed up Zac's arm.

Three babies were tumbling and rolling in the sand.

The meerkat jumped from her lap onto Zoe's head. Zoe dropped the bowl in surprise. Grubs went flying!

'Aaaah,' cried Zoe. Four meerkats jumped onto Zoe's lap, scrambling for food.

'Looks like the meerkats
want to cuddle *you*,' joked Zac.

'I've had enough of
meerkats,' said Zoe. 'What's
next?'

Chapter 4

Elephant Poo

'Next, we'll help Tom clean out the elephant barn,' said Mum. 'It's a *huge* mess.'

Mum pushed the wheelbarrow into the barn. Zoe and Zac carried shovels.

Tom, the elephant keeper,
was scrubbing the water
trough.

'Whoa! Six elephants make
a lot of poo,' said Zac.

'About 70 kilos for each
elephant,' said Zoe.

Zoe scooped up a big pile and threw it in the wheelbarrow. Zac scooped another pile. It was hot, hard, *stinky* work.

Through the open doorway, they could see the elephants paddling in the pond in the paddock next door.

A baby elephant called Kye sprayed his brother with water. Tye sprayed him back.

Kye flopped in the water, trumpeting loudly.

Tye dropped in the mud and rolled.

Zoe and Zac giggled.

'Elephants love swimming and splashing,' said Zoe.

Tye put his trunk in the
pond and sucked in water. He
stretched out his trunk and
blew. Water sprayed over the
fence. Soaking Zoe and Zac.

Tye flapped his ears with delight. He looked like he was laughing.

'*Tye*,' cried Zac. He wiped his face. 'Naughty elephant!'

'I'm *soaked*,' said Zoe. 'And muddy!'

'Never mind,' said Mum. 'You'll dry.'

When the barn was clean, Zoe felt tired and dirty. Zoo work was *not* how she'd imagined it. But there was no time to rest. Mum wanted to check on Amali.

Chapter 5

Where's Amali?

Zoe and Zac jumped out of the jeep and raced to the fence.

'Where's Amali?' asked Zac.

'I can't see her,' said Zoe.

Zulu roared.

Mum looked worried.

'Do you think she's escaped?' asked Zoe.

'Maybe she's hurt or sick.' Zac searched through his binoculars.

Where could Amali be?

'We'd better take a closer look,' said Mum. 'I'm sure she's just hiding.'

'Do you mean go inside?' asked Zoe. Her heart thumped. 'With the *lions*?'

Chapter 6

Into the Lions' Den

'We'll be safe in the jeep,'
said Mum.

Mum wound up the
windows.

They drove through the
safety gates and into the lion
enclosure.

Zac checked left and right
with his binoculars.

Amali wasn't skulking
in the rocks. She wasn't
snoozing under a log. She
wasn't even snooping among
the trees.

Zoe saw a tiny movement in the rushes by the waterhole. Was it the wind?

'Over there,' said Zoe. 'Is that her?'

Zac checked. 'No, nothing,' he said. There was another flicker. 'Wait. I can see . . . ears!'

Mum drove over and parked the jeep. Nothing moved. Mum frowned.

Zoe felt worried.

Zac kept searching.

'Look!' He handed Zoe the binoculars.

Zoe took a moment to find it. Then she saw something amazing.

Chapter 7

Amali's Surprise

The rushes had been
flattened to make a nest.
Lying there was Amali.
Cuddled up to her side
were two tiny lion cubs.

They were still damp with
their eyes tightly shut.

Amali licked them gently.

'She's had babies!' said Zoe.

'They're *so cute*,' said Zac.

'I want to cuddle them.'

Mum peered through the binoculars.

'Those cubs weren't due for another week. Lions are endangered in the wild, so cubs born in zoos are very special,' said Mum. She put down the binoculars. 'The work we do at the zoo is important. We protect lots of species, so they don't become extinct.'

Zoe felt proud of her mum and the other zookeepers.

'We'd better tell the vet,' said Mum. 'She'll want to check the babies.'

'What are you going to call them?' asked Zac.

'I think our cubs need special names.' Mum winked. 'I think we should call them . . . Zoe and Zac – after two very special new zookeepers.'

Zoe and Zac grinned at each other.

'This has been the best day *ever*,' said Zac. 'We're so lucky to live in a zoo!'

'Absolutely,' said Zoe.
'I wouldn't want to live
anywhere else in the world.'

Fun Facts
About Animals

Wombats sleep during the daytime. They come outside to eat grass and roots at night.

Lions are large cats that live in groups called prides. The pride is headed by the main lioness. Male lions guard the cubs while the lionesses hunt. Lions spend up to 21 hours a day napping.

Meerkats have dark circles around their eyes to protect them from the sun. Meerkats look cute but they can kill a python!

Giraffes are the tallest mammals on earth. Each giraffe has its own unique spots. Giraffes only sleep for 5 to 30 minutes per day, usually standing up!

About the AUTHOR

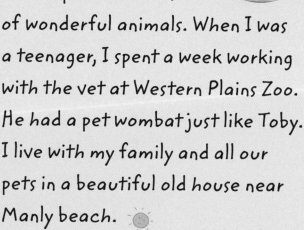

I grew up in a
vet hospital with lots
of wonderful animals. When I was
a teenager, I spent a week working
with the vet at Western Plains Zoo.
He had a pet wombat just like Toby.
I live with my family and all our
pets in a beautiful old house near
Manly beach.

About the ILLUSTRATOR

Ever since I was a child,
I loved drawing and
always went everywhere with
a pencil and paper.

Like Zoe and Zac, I love animals
and have always enjoyed going to the
zoo and drawing them. ☺

Tick the Aussie Kids books you have read:

Meet Zoe and Zac at the Zoo
Belinda Murrell & David Hardy

Meet Taj at the Lighthouse
Maxine Beneba Clarke & Nicki Greenberg

Meet Eve in the Outback
Raewyn Caisley & Karen Blair

Meet Katie at the Beach
Rebecca Johnson & Lucia Masciullo

Meet Sam at the Mangrove Creek
Paul Seden & Brenton McKenna

Meet Mia by the Jetty
Janeen Brian & Danny Snell

Meet Dooley on the Farm
Sally Odgers

Meet Matilda at the Festival
Jacqueline de Rose-Ahern